TOM the OBSCURE

First published in Great Britain 2013

Copyright © 2013 by Lucy Ellmann

The moral right of the author has been asserted

All artwork © Lucy Ellmann

Bloomsbury Publishing plc
50 Bedford Square
London
WC1B 3DP

www.bloomsbury.com

Bloomsbury Publishing, London, New Delhi, New York and Sydney

A CIP catalogue record for this book is available from the British Library

ISBN 978 1 4088 4578 3

10 9 8 7 6 5 4 3 2 1

Typeset by Aaron Munday (12 Orchards)

Printed in Great Britain by LDA, Berkshire

TOM the OBSCURE

Lucy Ellmann

BLOOMSBURY
LONDON · NEW DELHI · NEW YORK · SYDNEY

Bloomsbury Publishing was given over to the life of the mind. The entire building was adorned, insulated and overwhelmed by books.

The receptionist sat in a vast book-lined drawing room. Tea was made in a rudimentary kitchen area. There was one tiny loo for all.

But there was food around somewhere. Having only recently moved to Bedford Square from Soho, the staff at Bloomsbury had eclectic tastes, from Italian sweetmeats, Chinese pork buns and Thai noodle dishes, to sausage rolls, samosas and turquoise macaroons. The editorial department's snack pile was almost as big as its slush pile! And these delicacies resulted in a wide variety of crumbs.

For every crumb, a mouse is born. Mice are the unpaid crumb gardeners of the world. They come, unbidden and misunderstood, to tend to things.

Mice have a sense of order. They *must*: their babies are born tiny, blind and bare! Things have to be ship-shape when such infants appear.

The mice got to work, raking, composting and cultivating the colourful crumbs. There were so many titbits, they called for reinforcements, and even had a camouflage unit, which set up many dummy crumb piles and decoy mouse holes.

Into this mousey *coup d'état* came Tom,
a marvellous heathen of a ginger farm cat,
who'd never seen a book in his life.

He began well, wrestling energetically with
his victims amongst manuscripts on Achilles,
Mauritius and San Miguel. He hid behind
piles of non-fiction, awaiting battle; he
relaxed and cleansed himself on fiction. But
his efforts were frequently interrupted by
meetings, always the meetings! *Meow!*

A difficult author brought her dog in one day
and the uncultured mutt immediately grasped
Tom's head in its jaws – but Tom was rescued
and the author's publicity budget much reduced.

Only once was Tom taken outside for a walk
in Bedford Square – on a lead! It was shameful
to appear there *like a dog*, but when he dashed
up a tree the lead was mercifully dropped.

From a high branch in the growing dusk, Tom
caught sight of the British Pregnancy Advisory
Service, which made him think mournfully
of his own limited chance of romance (no
other cats seemed to come to this park).

But after many pleas from below, and threats of firemen, Tom parachuted down from bough to bough, legs outstretched to slow his fall.

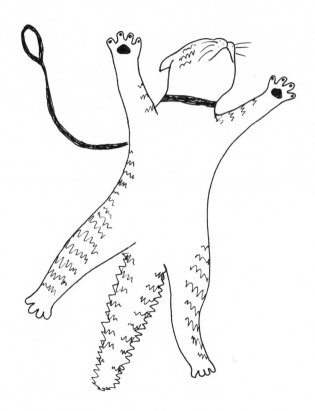

Tom was all settled in at Bloomsbury.
The trouble was, he forgot about the mice!
He patrolled the offices not for rodents,
but for legs to rub against and hands
to tickle his ears. Designers, production
managers, publicists, marketers, accountants,
editors, assistant editors, cleaners and
assistant cleaners clandestinely fed him.

At night, he slept soundly in an armchair in
the reception room, awaiting human contact,
while the mice scooted around upstairs, digging,
pruning, harvesting, feasting, and developing
grand landscaping schemes. (And reading!)

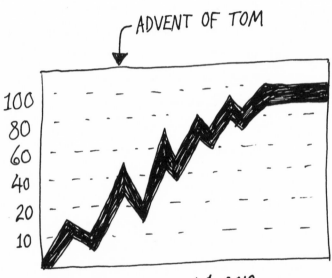

Mouse Figures, Chart 1, 2012

22

A meeting was held to assess mouse figures and the effectiveness of Tom. Some people, allergic to cats, were starting to sneeze. Others (dog lovers, no doubt) argued for the practicality of mousetraps. A copy-editor spoke up eloquently for *mice*. But even his supporters had to admit that Tom had a bad habit of crapping on forthcoming titles.

'Don't you see what we've got here?' said Alexandra Pringle finally. 'He's not a mouser, he's an intellectual. We turned a farm boy into a philosopher. This cat is Tom the Obscure. Send him to Oxford!'

Tom did well at Oxford. He lived in a bed-sit in Jericho, well stocked with mice, and on this frugal but high-protein diet completed his doctorate: 'The Existential, Epistemic, Epistemological, Ontological, Logical, Logistical and Oogenetic Impediments to the Execution of Feline Reproductive Rites Amongst Confined Cats in and around Bedford Square'.

On his return to Bloomsbury for work experience, Tom founded an exciting new imprint – Bloomsbury Paw Print – specialising in cat books. Tom was now a publishing hepcat, and spent his nights on the town. And he kindly enlisted the mice of the editorial department as a vast proofreading army, in recognition of their creditable attention to detail.

by Lucy Ellmann
Editor and Production Assistant: Todd McEwen